**Teggs is no ordinary dinosaur—
he's an astrosaur!**

Captain of the amazing spaceship DSS *Sauropod*, he goes on dangerous missions, fighting evil with the help of his faithful crew, Gipsy, Arx, and Iggy!

Read all the adventures of
Captain Teggs and his crew!

Book One: *Riddle of the Raptors*

Book Two: *The Hatching Horror*

Coming Soom
Book Four: *The Mind-Swap Menace*

The Seas of Doom

BY STEVE COLE

ILLUSTRATED BY WOODY FOX

Aladdin Paperbacks
New York • London • Toronto • Sydney

For Annie and James

ALADDIN PAPERBACKS
An imprint of Simon & Schuster Children's Publishing Division
1230 Avenue of the Americas, New York, NY 10020
Text copyright © 2005 by Steve Cole
Map copyright © 2005 by Charlie Fowkes
Illustrations copyright © 2005 by Woody Fox
Originally published in Great Britain in 2005 by Red Fox, an imprint of Random House Children's Books
Published by arrangement with Rocket Editorial Ltd.
First U.S. edition 2006
All rights reserved, including the right of reproduction in whole or in part in any form.
ALADDIN PAPERBACKS and colophon are trademarks of Simon & Schuster, Inc.
Designed by Steve Kennedy
The text of this book was set in ITC Legacy Serif Book.
Manufactured in the United States of America
First Aladdin Paperbacks edition October 2006
10 9 8 7 6 5 4 3 2
Library of Congress Control Number 2006921814
ISBN-13: 978-0-689-87843-5
ISBN-10: 0-689-87843-5

WARNING!

THINK YOU KNOW ABOUT DINOSAURS?

THINK AGAIN!

The dinosaurs . . .

Big, stupid lumbering reptiles. Right?

All they did was eat, sleep, and roar a bit. Right?

Died out millions of years ago when a big meteor struck Earth. Right?

Wrong!

The dinosaurs weren't stupid. They may have had small brains, but they used them well. They had big thoughts and big dreams.

By the time the meteor hit, the last dinosaurs had already left Earth forever. Some species had discovered how to travel through space as early as the Triassic period, and were already enjoying a new life among the stars.

No one has found evidence of dinosaur technology yet. But the first fossil bones were found only in 1787, and new finds are being made all the time. The proof is out there, buried in the ground.

And the dinosaurs live on, way out in space, even now. They've settled down in a place they call the Jurassic Quadrant, and over the last sixty-five million years they've continued to evolve. . . .

The dinosaurs we'll be meeting are part of a special group called the Dinosaur Space

 Service. Their job is to explore space, to go on exciting missions, and to fight evil and protect the innocent!

These heroic herbivores are not just dinosaurs.

They are *astrosaurs*!

NOTE: *The following story has been translated from secret Dinosaur Space Service records. Earthling dinosaur names are used throughout, although some changes have been made for easy reading.*

THE CREW OF THE DSS SAUROPOD

Captain
Teggs Stegosaur

Arx Orano,
first officer

Gipsy Saurine,
communications
officer

Iggy Tooth,
chief engineer

Jurassic Quadrant

Ankylos

Steggos

Diplox

INDEPENDENT
DINOSAUR
ALLIANCE

vegetarian
sector

Squawk
Major

DSS
UNION OF
PLANETS

PETROSAURI

Corytho

Lambeos

Tri System

Iguanos

Aqua Minor

SEA

OUTER SPACE

Geldos Cluster

Teerex Major

Olympus

TYRANNOSAUR TERRITORIES

Planet Sixty

carnivore sector

Raptos

THEROPOD EMPIRE

Megalos

vegmeat zone
(neutral space)

LE SPACE

Pliosaur Nurseries

Not to scale

Chapter One

A SOGGY MISSION

In orbit high above the planet Aqua Minor, Captain Teggs Stegosaur was waiting to start his next adventure.

He was waiting *very* impatiently.

"Admiral Rosso had better call us soon," Teggs grumbled, chomping on the delicious moss that covered his control pit. "I can't wait to find out why we've been sent to the soggiest planet in the Jurassic Quadrant."

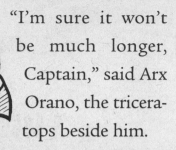

"I'm sure it won't be much longer, Captain," said Arx Orano, the triceratops beside him.

Sitting around twiddling his thumbs wasn't easy for the young, daredevil stegosaurus. He didn't have any thumbs, for one thing.

Teggs commanded the DSS *Sauropod*, the finest ship in the Dinosaur Space Service. He and his crew were all highly trained astrosaurs. They flew through space helping plant-eaters in peril—wherever the planet, whatever the risk.

But why had the *Sauropod* been sent to a world full of *fish*?

"Maybe Admiral Rosso thinks we need a holiday by the seaside," said Iggy Tooth, the *Sauropod*'s chief engineer. A brave iguanodon, he

was good with machines and fiercely loyal to his captain. "I don't really like the seaside. I'm not keen on fish. I met a fish with no eyes once."

"That would make it a *fsh*. Get it?" called Gipsy Saurine from her seat. Gipsy was a duck-billed hadrosaur with scaly, stripy skin. She handled the ship's communications and much more besides. "Anyway, there *is* no sea-side on Aqua Minor. Only sea."

"Calling Captain Teggs." The gruff voice of Admiral Rosso, the crusty old barosaurus in charge of the Dinosaur Space Service, suddenly crackled from the *Sauropod*'s speakers. "Captain Teggs, can you hear me?"

"At last!" spluttered Teggs through a mouthful of moss. He rose from the control pit, and now the crew could see his entire body—eight meters long from tail to beak, with jagged bony plates running down his orange-brown back.

Gipsy Saurine trotted over to Teggs. "Shall I put the admiral on the scanner screen, Captain?" she asked.

"Yes, please," said Teggs.

Gipsy whistled the order through her snout to the dimorphodon. These plucky pterosaurs were the *Sauropod*'s flight crew, and they loved to be bossed around.

The team leader flapped down and pecked the scanner control happily with his beak. A moment later, Admiral Rosso's wrinkled face appeared.

"Ah, there you are, Teggs," said the old barosaurus. "Sorry to keep you waiting, but running an entire space fleet keeps me busy. And when you get to my age . . ."

Teggs saluted. "What's up, sir?"

"It's what's *down* that's worrying us," said Admiral Rosso. "Down below!"

Arx and Gipsy swapped puzzled looks. But Teggs just smiled at the thought of a brand-new adventure at last.

"Something very big and very dangerous is swimming around in the seas of Aqua Minor," the admiral went on. "The cryptoclidus who fish there are getting very worried."

Teggs frowned. "Crypto-who?"

"A race of sea reptiles from the planet Cryptos," Arx explained. "They have run out of food in their own world, so now they fish the waters of Aqua Minor for squid and shellfish. Then they send it by rocket to the folks back home."

"Very good, Arx." Admiral Rosso smiled. "Teggs, you have a first-rate first officer there!"

"He's the best," Teggs agreed. "So what's been happening on Aqua Minor?"

"Five undersea fish factories have been wrecked, along with several submarines." Admiral Rosso sighed. "But no one knows who's doing it—or why."

Teggs nodded. "And you want us to find out."

"That's right," said Admiral Rosso. "The cryptoclidus may not be vegetarians, but they are still our friends and neighbors in space. They've asked us for help in solving this mystery."

"So what are we waiting for?" asked Teggs. "Let's get to Aqua Minor and see what we can find!"

Once Admiral Rosso had given them a map and some orders, Teggs, Gipsy, and Arx went to the shuttle bay. The air was smoky and thick with the smell of the burning dung that fueled the engines. Iggy Tooth was waiting for them by the shuttle.

"The engines are all fired up, Captain!" said the stocky iguanodon. "We're ready to go!"

Once they were all safely strapped in, the shuttle blasted off. Soon they were soaring through the brilliant blue skies of Aqua Minor.

"Wow!" said Teggs, peering through the window. "What a view. There's nothing to see but sea!"

Below them, the green ocean stretched out endlessly to the horizon. Enormous spaceships floated above the waves, trailing fishing nets behind them. Teggs watched one spaceship rise higher than the rest. Its net was bulging with shimmering, silvery shellfish that sparkled in the bright sunlight.

"No wonder the cryptoclidus need our help,"

said Arx. "This is a very big ocean for something nasty to hide in."

"Where are we going to park the shuttle?" asked Iggy.

"On one of their floating factories," said Gipsy, checking her wrist tracker. "It's not far from here."

"It was the first place to be attacked," said Teggs. "We'll take a look and search for clues."

Soon the floating factory came into sight.

It looked like a large square of shiny metal, covered in long huts. In the middle of the square, a small gray shape started waving at them.

"Who's that?" asked Iggy as they came in to land.

"That must be Commander Cripes," said Arx. "He'll be showing us around."

The shuttle landed safely, and its doors slid

open. A strong smell of salty fish
filled the air.

As the dinosaurs stepped outside, Cripes came waddling
up to greet them. Like all
cryptoclidus, he looked
like a cross between a
seal and the Loch Ness
Monster. He had a long
neck and four flat flippers, and
his belly dragged on the ground as
he moved. A broad-brimmed hat was perched
on his head, and a shiny cape kept the sun off
his long, smooth back.

"Welcome to Aqua Minor, guys," said Cripes.
"Admiral Rosso said you were on your way.
Glad you could make it!"

"Thanks," said Teggs. "This is Arx, and this
is Iggy."

Cripes smiled. "And this cute little hadrosaur just *has* to be Gipsy." He took her hoof in

his flipper and kissed it. "Now, let me show you around. This factory stretches down almost to the seabed. . . ."

Cripes led them into a hut and then into a large elevator. It took them down deep under the water. When it finally stopped, Teggs led the way out into a large, crumbling workplace. The machines and conveyor belts stood silent. The walls were cracked. The floor was flooded with smelly, oily water.

"Hard to believe that this place was brand-new six weeks ago, isn't it?" Cripes sighed. "Just two weeks after opening, *this* happened."

Teggs stared around. "Something has torn the whole place apart!"

"And this was just the first attack," Cripes reminded him. "In the last month there have been lots more. Every new factory we build in this area gets wrecked!"

"What are they used for, anyway?" asked Gipsy.

"The floating factories prepare the fish we catch before we send it back home to feed our people," Cripes explained. "On the bottom levels, we suck in thousands of ammonites and belemnites from the pens on the sea bed. We take off the shells and rinse them clean. And then a submarine delivers them here for packaging."

"We're under the sea, aren't we?" asked Iggy. "So how come this place isn't full of water?"

"We cryptoclidus live on land as well as in the sea," Cripes reminded him. "The food is easier to pack when it's not floating around all over the place."

Arx plodded over to a wall and prodded a button with his longest horn. Everyone jumped as the machines sparked into life. The conveyor belt jerked forward. Metal scoops swung down from the wonky ceiling.

"Cool—the machines still work!" Teggs shouted over all the noise. "What do they do?"

"The fish plop out of this pipe here onto the conveyor belt," Cripes explained over the noise. "Then they're wrapped up in the wrapping machine and sent upstairs to the spaceships. But nothing has come through that pipe for weeks, and in the meantime, the people back home are going hungry."

Teggs felt sad watching the ruined machines clanking away with no purpose. But before he could turn them off, he felt the ground shake beneath his feet.

"That's not the builders starting work on the

repairs already, is it?" asked Gipsy nervously.

Suddenly the whole factory rocked as if a giant had kicked it. The astrosaurs were knocked off their feet. The cracks in the walls widened. The floor broke open beneath them, and seawater began rushing in.

"Never mind the builders!" cried Teggs over the noise of the machines and the churning water. "I think the thing that attacked this place before has come back to finish it off!"

Chapter Two

THE SINISTER SHADOW

"Quick, you guys!" yelled Cripes. "Back to the elevator!"

Iggy and Gipsy didn't need telling twice. They quickly splashed over to the elevator. Teggs and Arx began to follow. But before they could reach the others, the floor before them crumbled away into the water.

"We're cut off!" cried Arx.

"Iggy! Gipsy!" shouted Teggs. "Get out of here now, while you can!"

"But we can't leave you!" called Gipsy. "You'll drown!"

"That's an order!" Teggs bellowed.

Iggy sadly saluted him, and Cripes pressed a button. The elevator clanked slowly upward.

"We'll get help!" Gipsy called. Then they were gone.

Arx yelped as a large chunk of falling ceiling nearly squashed him. "Come away from the edge, Captain!" he shouted. "If you fall down there, you'll never get out again!"

"Wait!" Teggs called, rooted to the spot. "Look! Something's moving down there!"

Arx edged closer. Sure enough, he saw a dark shadow in the oily water. It looked like the shadow of something very big and very, very dangerous.

"If only we could get a closer look at it," said Teggs.

"Captain," Arx gasped, "if the water level

keeps rising, *it* might swim up here to get a closer look at *us*!"

Together they backed away from the edge. The freezing cold water was now up to their chins.

"This looks like the end." Arx sighed.

"We'll find a way out," said Teggs bravely. He tried to think, but it wasn't easy with the noise of the clanking machines all around him.

Then he had a brainwave.

"The machines!" he cried. "If we can climb up onto the machines, we'll be higher up. The water will take longer to reach us!"

Teggs grabbed hold of one of the dangling scoops with his beak. He used it to haul him-

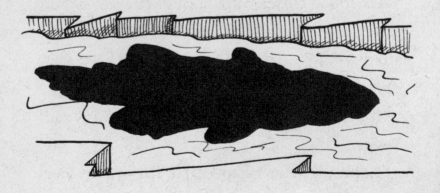

self up onto the clanking conveyor belt. Arx tried to do the same, but he struggled. Teggs wrapped his tail round the triceratops's head frill and helped him up.

"Now the water only comes up to our toes!" Teggs beamed.

"But we're heading for the wrapping machine!" cried Arx. "It'll squash us up into a parcel!"

"No, it won't," said Teggs, smashing his big, bony tail into the machine. It exploded in a cloud of sparks. "I think it's out of order." He grinned.

As the sparks died away, the machines suddenly stopped. The room fell eerily quiet. The only sound was the swoosh of the seawater beneath them.

"I guess I caused a short circuit," said Teggs.

"At least we can hear ourselves think now," said Arx. He paused. "Er, Captain . . . can you hear what I hear?"

Teggs listened. "I can't hear anything."

"Exactly," said Arx. "Whatever was attacking us seems to have given up."

Teggs peered over the edge of the conveyor belt. There was no sign of the dark shadow beneath the sea. "I think you're right," he whispered.

But then something large and white came whizzing up through the water.

"Look out!" yelled Teggs.

The big white thing burst out of the sea below them with a massive splash. A huge wave of water crashed over Teggs and Arx, blinding them both.

"It's a sea monster!" shouted Arx, blinking furiously.

"Get behind me, Arx!" cried Teggs, his eyes stinging. "I'll fight it off!"

"Actually," said a familiar voice, "I only wanted to give you a lift."

Teggs grinned with delight as he blinked

away the last of the saltwater. "Iggy!" he cried.

The big white thing was only the shuttle. Now it bobbed about on the water in front of them, like a giant rubber duck in a very big bath. Iggy stood in the doorway.

Gipsy leaned out behind him and waved.

"We thought this might be a good time to see if the shuttle works underwater."

"Luckily it does," added Cripes, peering over Gipsy's shoulder. "At least for short trips."

"Good work, guys," said Teggs as he leaped aboard. "Come on, there's no time to lose. We just saw something very big and dark swimming about down here. Let's try to follow it."

"That's risky, Captain," said Arx. "That thing must be big enough to swallow the shuttle in one gulp!"

"It's a risk we'll have to take," Teggs told him.

Once Arx had scrambled into the shuttle, they set off. Like a submarine, the little ship ducked under the waves and hummed quietly through the clear green water. But all they saw were schools of tiny fish swimming past them. There was no sign of the mysterious dark thing.

"How could it just vanish?" Teggs asked.

Suddenly a warning light came on in the shuttle.

"Seawater's getting into the engine pipes," said Iggy.

"Okay, Iggy." Teggs sighed. "Better head back to the surface, fast!"

"Aye, aye, Captain," said Iggy.

He steered the shuttle sharply upward. A few

seconds later, it burst from the sea like a great white whale. The warning light went out, and everyone breathed a sigh of relief.

Teggs turned to Cripes. "Is there somewhere we can go to plan our next move?"

"The nearest base is Sea Station One, fifty miles north of here. It's where the fishing teams live while they're staying on Aqua Minor."

"Will the shuttle get us that far?" asked Arx.

"Just about," said Iggy. "We don't have enough power to fly, but we can chug along the surface like a motorboat."

"Good," said Teggs with a grin. "I just hope there will be some food there. I'm *starving*!"

Chapter Three

DEEP DOWN DANGER

"Wow!" said Gipsy as the shuttle sailed into sight of Sea Station One. It was like a cross between a grand hotel, a beautiful harbor, and a busy spaceport. Some cryptoclidus were splashing about in enormous pools of salty water. Others sat in water-filled cafés eating buckets of fish.

In the distance, rockets blasted off from the floating factories, filled with food to take home to Cryptos. And as Gipsy followed her friends off the shuttle, a large fishing boat pulled into the sea station, filled with groups of chattering cryptoclidus.

She turned to Cripes. "What do you need old-fashioned fishing boats for? I thought you had spaceships to pull your nets."

"The boats take our workers to and from the floating factories," Cripes explained. "Few of us dare to swim in the sea at the moment."

"Well, we'll have to *sea* what we can do about that," Teggs said, chuckling.

"Have you marked where the monster attacks took place?" asked Arx.

Cripes took out a map of Aqua Minor from

28

his raincoat and Gipsy helped him unfold it. "*X* marks the spot," he said. "*Several* spots."

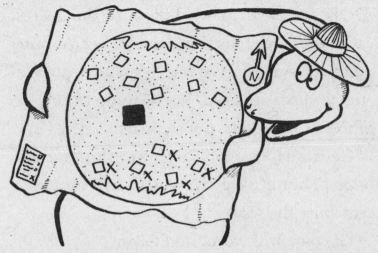

"So all five attacks took place in the southern part of the planet," noted Arx.

"That's right," said Cripes. "All our other floating factories are in the north. We've been trying to build new ones in the south to meet the demand for shellfish back home—"

"But every single one has been destroyed," growled Iggy.

"It looks like someone—or something—is fed up with you fishing here," said Gipsy.

"And it's our job to find out who," said Teggs bravely. "Once we've had a quick snack . . ."

"Of course." Cripes led them to the nearest café and slapped his flippers together. A waiter paddled straight over with a massive plate of sticky, slimy seaweed. Teggs took a cautious nibble. It tasted like wet salty dishcloths.

"Delicious," gasped Teggs weakly. "But perhaps I should skip the snack. I should start searching the sea."

"I'll come with you," said Gipsy.

"You know it's risky," Cripes warned them.

"Of course." Teggs beamed. "But if we're to help you, we need to find out more."

"I wish I could let you guys take a sub," said Cripes. "But we don't have any left. We tried looking for the monster in them. But the subs are so noisy, I guess the monster heard us coming a mile away. It chewed them all up!"

Gipsy looked worried. "Did the pilots get out?"

"Only just," said Cripes. "But by the time they they'd wriggled out of the wrecks, there was no sign of the monster at all." He clicked his tongue. "Oh, well. Maybe you'll have more luck in the diving bell."

"What's a diving bell?" asked Teggs.

"It's a big metal case with a window on the side," Arx explained. "It'll take you underwater."

"We take you out to sea," said Cripes. "Then we lower you down into the water on a chain so you can take a good look around."

"How will we breathe?" asked Teggs.

"It's completely airtight," Cripes assured him. "But there's also deep-sea diving gear on board in case of emergencies."

"What if we get into trouble?" asked Gipsy.

"Just press the help button," said Cripes. "We'll have you back out again in no time!"

"Fair enough," said Teggs. "Meanwhile, I'd like Arx to check over those chewed-up subs for clues."

"No problem," Cripes told him. "They're all piled up in a storeroom downstairs."

"Can I see some wreckage from the floating factory, too?" asked Arx.

"We'll pick some up for you." Cripes rose and adjusted his hat. "Well, if you guys are ready . . ."

"We sure are!" Teggs jumped to his feet. "Let's get going!"

Cripes took them out in one of the big fishing boats to the wreck of the floating factory. Teggs was wearing his battle armor, and Gipsy had slipped on her combat suit.

"I've never tried using my electro-tail underwater," said Teggs thoughtfully.

"Arx said our armor would work wherever we were," said Gipsy. "And if we do meet any monsters down there, I'm glad about that!"

Once they had reached the wreck, Teggs and Gipsy squeezed inside the orange diving bell. There was just room for the two of them and the diving gear.

Cripes waved at them through the window. "On top of the bell is a special camera," he said. "It can see through murky water. So if you do find a nasty sea monster down there, we should get a good picture of it."

"We'll ask it to say 'cheese,'" joked Teggs.

"Good luck, guys," said Cripes. Iggy pressed a big green button, and Gipsy squealed as the bell was heaved up over the side of the ship on heavy chains.

"This is better than a funfair ride!" Teggs declared. He looked out through the large window in the side of the bell. On the ship's deck, Iggy stood beside Cripes. He gave a small, worried wave to his captain.

Slowly the diving bell was lowered into the water. Teggs and Gipsy were soon staring out at an undersea world. Curious fish swam up to see them.

Deeper and deeper they went. A friendly octopus blinked at them as it drifted by. A strange, spindly fish spiraled lazily past.

The bell came to rest on the seabed with a soft bump. The water through the window was cloudy and dark. Nothing moved. Nothing stirred at all.

Gipsy felt a shiver go through her. "I hope this thing doesn't leak," she said.

Teggs nodded. "Let's put on the diving gear, just in case."

They opened the trunk, and helped each other strap oxygen tanks on their backs. Then they put on special diving helmets.

"Now we'll be ready for anything." Teggs said.

But neither of them was ready for what happened next.

Wham!

The diving bell shook with an enormous blow.

"What was that?" gasped Gipsy.

"I don't know!" said Teggs. He peered out the window—and wished he hadn't.

A massive sea monster with huge, yellow eyes was staring at them. Its skin was a deep blotchy blue and white. Its head was the size of a sofa and the top of it was wrapped in a tattered bandage. It was easily three times as long as Teggs, and its flippers were the size of small trees.

The sea monster smiled, revealing a long row of terrifying teeth. Then it attacked the diving bell. Its teeth tore through the metal like wet cardboard. Seawater flooded in through the gaping hole in the wall.

"Hit the help button, Gipsy!" cried Teggs. "It's coming to get us!"

Chapter Four

THE MONSTER

Up on the ship, the chain holding the diving bell was swinging about like a piece of string in a gale.

"Something's wrong!" gasped Iggy. "Quick! Bring up the bell!"

Cripes hit a yellow button on his control panel. The chain clanked and heaved,

but the diving bell wouldn't rise.

"It's jammed!" cried Cripes. "Something's got hold of it!"

"I'll boost the power," said Iggy. He fiddled with some wires beneath the control panel. "Try it now!"

Cripes pressed the button again. This time, the bell began to move up from the seabed.

He beamed at Iggy. "You did it!"

Iggy and Cripes waited tensely. Finally the orange diving bell emerged from the foaming waters.

Or what was left of it.

The bell had been mangled and squashed. Half of it was missing altogether. But most worrying of all, it was completely empty.

"Teggs and Gipsy," Iggy whispered. "They've gone!"

"But so has their diving gear," said Cripes, peering inside. "Maybe they got away."

"If they did, they're still too heavy to swim up from the bottom of the sea!" wailed Iggy. "We have to find them fast!"

Cripes clapped his flippers. Two cryptoclidus sailors in white caps and overalls slithered up to him.

"We need to get a search party down there, guys," said Cripes. "Ten of your fastest swimmers, right now!"

The two sailors nodded. "Straightaway, sir," they cried, and then dashed off.

Iggy sighed, wishing the shuttle worked better underwater so he could look for himself. "How long can Teggs and Gipsy stay down there?"

"Let me see." Cripes counted on his flippers. "They should have enough air to last three hours. After that . . ."

Iggy looked very glum. "I suppose I'd better tell Arx the bad news," he said.

"We won't just tell him," said Cripes gravely. "We'll *show* him." He pointed a flipper at the mangled bell. "The undersea camera is still there. We'll take it back with us and see what happened."

"Well, what are we waiting for?" cried Iggy. "Let's get going!"

. . .

Iggy and Cripes found Arx busy working in the storeroom full of broken subs and wreckage from the floating factory. When the triceratops heard what had happened to the diving bell, his horns seemed to droop.

"Don't worry, Arx. The search party will find them and carry them safely back up to the surface," said Iggy stoutly. "Right, Cripes?"

"I sure hope so," said Cripes. He pulled out the camera from under his cape. "In the meantime, these pictures should be ready. Let's see what happened down there."

Arx and Iggy gathered round him as he pulled the back off the camera. Inside was a set of pictures, bone dry and crystal clear. Always impressed by a good invention, Arx was about to compliment Cripes on his clever camera. But he lost his voice when he saw what the pictures showed.

One showed the massive blue and white monster swimming up to the bell.

Another showed its enormous flippers and terrible tail.

"Look at the size of that thing!" gasped Cripes. "It's as big as a battleship!"

He quickly sorted through more of the pictures. They showed the monster grinning wildly, and then tearing through the thick metal of the diving bell. It seemed dead set on getting to Gipsy and Teggs.

"It should pick on someone its own size," said Iggy fiercely.

Cripes gulped. "There *is* no one else its own size!"

The second-to-last picture showed Teggs and Gipsy standing on the seabed in their diving gear. They were looking up at the fearsome creature.

"No!" Iggy groaned. "I don't want to see what happened next!"

"I'm afraid we must," said Arx quietly.

But the last of the pictures showed only the empty seabed.

"Where did they go?" demanded Iggy. "It's like they all just vanished!"

"At least there's no sign that they were hurt," said Cripes.

Arx nodded slowly. "And at least now we know that a liopleurodon is hiding down there in the deeps," he said.

Iggy frowned. "A what?"

"Back on Earth it was the biggest, nastiest killing machine in the water," Arx explained. "You're looking at one  hundred tons of swimming death."

"It . . . it can't be true!" stammered Cripes. "The liopleurodon rule those huge water worlds on the edge of the Jurassic Quadrant. No one's visited them for hundreds of years—they wouldn't dare!"

"Maybe not," said Arx darkly. "But it seems the liopleurodon have dared to visit Aqua Minor."

"If it *is* just a visit," growled Iggy. "This could be the start of an invasion!"

"But I don't understand." Cripes started shivering. "A liopleurodon ship couldn't land here without us knowing about it. And we've been fishing on Aqua Minor for five years without any trouble."

"Oh, come on! Wakey-wakey," cried Iggy. He waved the pictures in Cripes's face. "What more proof do you need? There's a liopleurodon down there! It's been smashing up your factories, eating your subs, and scaring everyone silly—and now it's got Teggs and Gipsy!"

Chapter Five

A STRANGE FRIEND

Back at the bottom of the sea, Teggs and Gipsy were facing up to the massive monster with the bandaged head.

Once the liopleurodon had ripped apart the diving bell, he floated in the water, watching them closely. Teggs had pulled his scariest face and swished his armored tail through the water. Gipsy was ready to jab their attacker on the nose if he came any closer.

But they were both surprised to find that the liopleurodon had no plans to eat them alive. In fact, he was very polite.

"Right, then!" he said brightly. Bubbles streamed out of his mouth as he spoke. "I've got you out of that horrible prison. Now you can come home with me!"

Teggs and Gipsy stared at each other in amazement through their diving helmets.

"What do you mean?" Gipsy cried. "That wasn't a prison!"

"Of course it was," said the liopleurodon. "You were both squished up inside, trapped by those flippery things. You were locked up and hanging from a chain. But now you're free!"

The sea monster smiled happily. He was clearly very pleased with himself.

Teggs turned to Gipsy. "What's a flippery thing?"

"It must be his word for the cryptoclidus," Gipsy whispered back.

Teggs cleared his throat. "Well, thanks for trying to help," he said. "But without that, er, *prison* as you call it, we can't get back up to the surface."

"Why would you want to do that?" asked the liopleurodon, baffled. "The flippery things would only lock you up again. No, no, we should stick together."

"What do you mean?" asked Gipsy.

"Well, *you're* not flippery things. *I'm* not a flippery thing. But everyone else on the planet *is*."

Teggs looked at him thoughtfully. "Who are you?"

"I think my name must be Mira," said the liopleurodon. "That's what is written on my outfit, anyway." He spun round to show them a torn scrap of blue uniform that clung to his middle. The word *MIRA* was spelled in gold thread.

"You mean you don't even know your own name?" asked Teggs.

"Nope!" said Mira cheerfully. "I must have been bumped on the head at some point. I'm sure I'm not just wearing this bandage because it looks pretty."

"That's for sure," murmured Gipsy.

"Anyway," said Mira, "now that I've set you free, you must help me find my spaceship. I'm sure I parked it around here somewhere, but that was a long, long time ago." He gave a sad little sigh. "I've been searching ever since."

"You parked a spaceship under the sea?" Teggs turned to Gipsy. "Bump on the head or not, this so-called sea monster is a nut!" he hissed.

Gipsy nodded. "But he's a very big, very dangerous nut with *extremely* big teeth," she

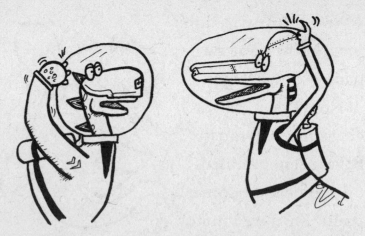

pointed out. "We'd better not upset him."

"Well?" asked Mira gravely. His gleaming eyes narrowed a little. "*Are* you going to help me?"

Teggs gulped. "Um . . . yes."

"Hurrah!" cried Mira, brightening again. "I know it's round here somewhere. We're bound to find it soon. Follow me!"

Gipsy cleared her throat. "Actually, I think we should stay here—"

"Follow me!" Mira yelled crossly, cutting her off. "My cave is this way."

Teggs and Gipsy couldn't move very fast

underwater. They shivered in the awful cold. Their heavy bodies ached as they trudged through the thick dark sand.

"We have to get back to the surface," muttered Gipsy. "We don't have enough air to stay down here for long."

"I know," said Teggs. "But how?"

Mira kept swimming around them in a big circle. "Keep up!" he yelled. "I can't wait to show you my cave! It's ever so cozy, and you'll

love the colors! I've chosen brown rock, with bits of darker brown rock and just a hint of very, *very* brown rock. . . ."

"This Mira is as batty as a belemnite," said Teggs quietly. "But he seems friendly enough."

Gipsy nodded. "So why has he been attacking factories and submarines?"

"What?" asked Mira, zooming up behind them. "Me? Attack factories and submarines? Why should I do that?"

"You tell us," said Teggs bravely. "That's what you've been doing, isn't it?"

"Don't be so silly," said Mira, floating upside down and going cross-eyed. "I've never attacked a factory in my life! I stay well away from those flippery things with their big nets. I don't want to get caught."

Gipsy turned back to Teggs. "Do you believe him?" she whispered.

"I don't know," said Teggs. "But why would he bother to lie? He could eat us alive in a couple of bites."

"Stop chatting and get a move on," nagged Mira. "Honestly, dinner will be ruined!"

Teggs perked up. "Dinner?"

"Yes!" cried Mira, waggling his flippers. "Din-dins! Come on! Come and get it!"

Teggs quickened his step. He was still starving.

"But *Captain*." Gipsy tapped his diving helmet with her hoof. "How are you going to eat through *that* thing?"

"Arrgh!" Teggs groaned. "I'm going as nutty as Mira!"

But when they finally reached the liopleurodon's lair, Teggs found he was glad to miss Mira's meal.

It was floating all about them in the cold, dark water—tons and tons of raw, rotten squid!

"Come on, chaps! Dig in!" Mira beamed. "Took me ages to catch this lot!"

"Oh." Gipsy swapped an awkward look

with Teggs. "Sorry, Mira, but we're, er, not really hungry."

"Not hungry?" Mira looked hurt. "But . . . I wanted to celebrate meeting you. I've been very lonely down here on my own, you know." Mira opened his giant jaws and gobbled down fifty squid in one single gulp. "So take those glass hats off your heads and eat up!"

"We can't," said Teggs.

"Of course you can," said Mira briskly. "No need to be shy."

"But we can't breathe underwater like you do," Teggs protested.

Mira folded his fins firmly. "Take them *off*!"

"We can't!" cried Gipsy. "If we do, we'll drown!"

"Drown? Don't be so silly," said Mira crossly. "Only the flippery things breathe air. *We* live in the sea." He came closer. "And if you won't take off those silly glass bubbles yourselves, I'll take them off for you!"

Mira's mouth swung open, revealing rows of lethal teeth, as he lunged toward them. . . .

Chapter Six

HIDE-AND-SEEK

Teggs and Gipsy dived out of the way just in time. Mira's razor sharp teeth scratched the side of Gipsy's glass helmet.

"Let me wear it, *please!*" she told Mira.

"What a lot of fuss you're making!" Mira tutted. "The silly thing doesn't even suit you!"

He opened his mouth again to pluck off Gipsy's

diving helmet. This time, he couldn't miss. . . .

Teggs flexed his armored tail, ready to whack Mira right on the flipper. But as his tail swung back it struck some rotten squid floating in the water. The power in his armor sparked through them. It made them glow electric pink in the gloomy cave.

Mira moaned in horror. "Ghosts!" he cried.

"My breakfast has come back to haunt me!" A cloud of bubbles burst from his behind. "Aaaaagh!"

With that, the terrified giant sped from the cave.

"What a brilliant plan, Captain!" said Gipsy admiringly. "But how did you know that using your electro-tail underwater would

light up anything it touched?"

Teggs stared at the glowing squid. He was almost as surprised as Mira. Then he grinned. "You know me, Gipsy," he said. "I may have a brain the size of an acorn, but I've always been a bright spark! Come on, let's get out of here before Mira comes back!"

They quickly left the cave. The water was dark and gloomy as they tried to retrace their steps across the seabed. But it was hard to tell which way they should go. At the bottom of the sea, everything looked the same—dark and spooky. Soon Teggs and Gipsy realized they were totally lost.

"We're running out of air, Captain," said Gipsy.

"Someone will find us soon!" Teggs said confidently.

"Yoo-hoo, crewmates!" came Mira's voice.

"Oh no," groaned Teggs. "I didn't mean *him*!"

"Hello?" The liopleurodon was getting closer. "Where are you?"

The two astrosaurs ducked down behind some clumps of seaweed.

"The ghosts have gone!" he shouted. "You can come back now!" Then his mouth opened in a big smile. "Oh, I see! It's a game! Hide-and-seek! Can't we play hunt the spaceship instead? I know it's round here some-where. . . ."

Mira swam closer, his massive head searching this way and that. Soon he would find them.

"Run for it!" hissed Teggs.

Together the two astrosaurs sprinted through the murky water. They slipped on slimy seaweed. Coral scraped their legs. Their sides ached with effort.

"Found you!" cried Mira close behind them. "You can't hide from me!"

"We have to keep going," gasped Teggs.

There was a big patch of slimy seaweed ahead. They slipped and skidded over it. Then, with a shout, Teggs fell *through* the seaweed!

Gipsy grabbed hold of his vanishing tail. She

tried to pull him back up, but he was too heavy. With a cry, Gipsy was dragged down through the slimy seaweed after him, into the blackness beyond.

The fall lasted only a few seconds. Teggs went tumbling through the water until he landed on his bottom with a bump. Gipsy landed beside him a second later. They were in a wide tunnel. Although the walls were thick with limpets and seaweed, something shiny was glinting through underneath.

Teggs took a closer look. "This isn't rock. It's metal!" he cried.

"A metal tunnel under the seabed?" Gipsy frowned. "What could it be?"

"Let's find out," he said. The astrosaurs walked cautiously along the tunnel, straining to see through the murky water. They came to a doorway. A sign glowed eerily above them: CONTROL ROOM.

Teggs nodded gravely. "I think we're inside a spaceship."

"*Mira's* spaceship," gasped Gipsy, "the one he's trying to find! But what's it doing here?"

"He didn't park it under the water," Teggs answered. "He must have crashed it into the ocean and right through the seabed. I think

we fell in through a big hole in the roof, hidden by the seaweed."

"But how do we get back out?" wondered Gipsy. "There's no way we can climb out of that hole again, and a search party would never think of looking for us down here. They don't even know this place exists!"

"And on top of that, our air is running out fast," said Teggs. "Cone on, Gipsy. Let's try to find another way back to the seabed."

Cautiously, they crept into the gloomy spaceship's control room.

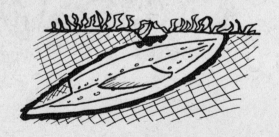

Chapter Seven

A TOOTHY RIDDLE

The sunken spaceship's control room was large and wide with a low ceiling. It was clearly designed for giant sea creatures. The controls were built into the floor, so the crew could work them with their tails and flippers.

Gipsy looked at a plastic newspaper floating in the water. "The *Liopluerodon Times*. It's six years old!" she said. "This ship has been down here for six whole years at the very least."

"So the ship crashed here a year before the cryptoclidus first arrived," Teggs realized. "And the trouble only started when they started building factories around this area."

"Maybe they disturbed something," said Gipsy. "Something dangerous."

Teggs nodded. Then he noticed a metal box on the floor with an aerial on top, half covered by the water. "Hey, Gipsy! This looks familiar."

"It's for sending distress calls," said Gipsy. "We've got something like it on the *Sauropod*."

She looked closely at the box. "It's broken . . . but maybe I can fix it."

"Try!" Teggs urged her. "If we could only send an SOS to Sea Station One . . ."

He waited anxiously while Gipsy went to work with her delicate claws. Finally she gave a small hoot of sadness. "I think I've got it working," she said. "But there's not much power. The signal is very weak."

"Someone will hear it," said Teggs quietly. "They *must*."

With nothing to do but wait, the

astrosaurs moved on into the cold shadows of the creepy ship.

Meanwhile, back on Sea Station One, Iggy and Arx were hard at work down in the storeroom. The two of them had been waiting ages for news of Teggs and Gipsy. They were worried sick.

Arx was still checking over the chewed-up wreckage. He was patiently comparing sections of sub, fragments of floating factory, and bits of the diving bell.

Iggy had talked some cryptoclidus sailors into helping him fix one of the broken subs. They were busy in the room next door, hammering out dents in the sub's metal body and fixing all the instruments. Iggy himself had taken tiny pieces from all the subs and was using them to build a brand-new engine. Now it was ready for testing, so he switched it on.

With a gentle hum, the engine started up on the first try.

"I've done it!" cried Iggy. "This new engine is ten times better and fifty times quieter than the old ones!"

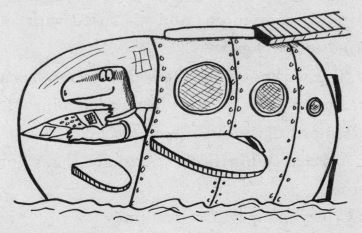

Then the door to the storeroom flew open as Cripes splashed inside.

Arx and Iggy spoke together. "Well?"

"The search party can't find a thing down there," said Cripes. "But every radio in the place is picking up some kind of weird SOS call. It seems to be coming from somewhere *beneath* the seabed!"

"It *might* be Teggs and Gipsy," cried Arx.

"If the captain and Gipsy are down there, I'll find them!" vowed Iggy. "My new supersub is almost ready to go. And it's fitted with all kinds of extra gadgets!"

"But we know that the liopleurodon has a taste for subs," Cripes reminded him. "It chomped all the old ones to pieces!"

Arx cleared his throat. "Actually, that's not true."

Cripes and Iggy stared at him.

"It was not a liopleurodon who chomped up the subs," he went on. "And it was not a liopleurodon who wrecked those floating factories."

"Come on!" Cripes scoffed. "You'll be telling us next that a liopleurodon didn't chew up that diving bell."

"Oh no," said Arx. "A liopleurodon *definitely* did that." He nodded. "That's how I know it didn't do anything else."

"How?" asked Cripes.

"Tooth marks!" cried Arx. "Look at that diving bell. It was ripped apart by long, sharp teeth. You can see the marks from here."

"So?" said Iggy.

"So, I haven't found tooth marks like that anywhere else," Arx said. "Not on *any* of this wreckage."

"What *did* you find?" asked Cripes.

"*Tiny* marks," Arx told him. "Hundreds of

thousands of tiny little marks—made by tiny *little* teeth!"

"But that's impossible," protested Iggy. "You and Captain Teggs both saw a huge shadow in the sea. That has to be the liopleurodon, right?"

"Maybe not," said Arx. "Maybe the liopleurodon is working with something else. Something just as big, or maybe even bigger!"

Cripes took off his hat and scratched his head with a flipper. "Strange for something so big to have such teeny-weeny teeth."

"Never mind that," said Iggy. "Let's get going!" He patted his shiny new engine. "We'll find Captain Teggs and Gipsy. And we'll find whatever else is hiding down there in the deeps, too—whatever it takes!"

Chapter Eight

THE FISH FACTOR

Back beneath the seabed, Teggs and Gipsy were still exploring the liopleurodon ship. It was cold, dark, and scary. And both of them knew that their precious air supply was running out with every breath they took. As they walked along one dark corridor, the dirty water grew chillier. The dirty water was becoming a thick, icy slush.

"Shall we turn back?" asked Gipsy nervously. "We don't want to wind up as dinosaur Popsicles!"

"Just a little farther," said Teggs.

The chilly passage ended in what seemed to be a giant freezer. Lying in the middle of the room were four big caskets made of solid ice. Teggs could see the huge dark shapes of lio-pleurodon lying inside three of them. But the fourth was damaged. Part of the ceiling had collapsed on top of it, and the casket had cracked right open.

"This must be Mira's crew," Gipsy gasped. "Are they dead?"

"Just sleeping, I think," Teggs said. "A deep, frozen sleep to keep them fresh while they wait to be rescued. But Mira's woken up ahead of time!"

Gipsy pointed to some blue scraps in the water beside the broken casket. "What are they?"

"Bits of Mira's uniform I think. There's writing on them." Teggs took a closer look. "*A* and *D* on this bit. An *L* on the other. What does that mean?"

"Admiral!" cried Gipsy.

Teggs frowned. "I'm only a captain at the moment!"

"No, I'm talking about Mira!" Gipsy's crest flushed red with excitement and made her helmet steam up. "He thought his name was Mira because it's written on that scrap of uniform he wears. But that's only *part* of the word. Really it spells AD—MIRA—L!"

"Of course!" Teggs exclaimed. "Then this really *is* his ship. But the ceiling fell in on his head before he could get into the deep freeze. That must be how he lost his memory!"

"Poor Mira." Gipsy sighed. "He must've slipped out into the sea in a daze, and forgotten how to get back."

"Yes—and something else may have slipped out with him," said Teggs quietly. "Let's keep looking."

"I wonder how much longer our air will last," said Gipsy. "We can't have much left by now."

"I know," said Teggs. "But we mustn't give up. An astrosaur fights on to the last breath!" He paused. "Sorry, that wasn't a very clever thing to say, was it?"

They left the chilly chamber and took a side tunnel. Soon they came to another room. It was marked LARDER—DO NOT DISTURB. A huge aquarium stretched along one wall for hundreds of meters. Nothing moved in the eerie, dark water.

"This must be where their food lived," said Gipsy.

Teggs was puzzled. "Strange to have an aquarium in a ship that's already full of water."

"I suppose the fish would swim all over the ship otherwise, trying to escape being eaten," Gipsy guessed. Then she noticed a big hole in the back of the tank. "Captain! The fish *did* escape! Look, they must have swum away into the sea!"

"Good for them." Teggs smiled. "I'm glad they got out." A thought struck him. "And if they did, maybe we can too! If we could find our way back out to the seabed, a search party might spot us."

"Brilliant!" cried Gipsy.

"All we have to do is break the glass. . . ." He struck the side of the tank with his tail. The glass glowed a brilliant blue and a crack appeared in its center.

Suddenly an alarm went off at earsplitting volume. Steel bars slammed down to block the doorway. They were trapped inside the larder!

"What did I do?" cried Teggs.

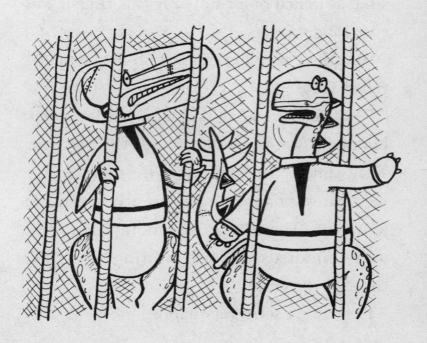

The siren stopped as a helpful computer voice chimed in from a speaker in the ceiling: "You tried to open the fish tank without a password. You are an intruder and fish stealer."

Teggs stared up at the speaker. "What would I do with a fish? I'm a vegetarian!"

"A likely story!" snarled the computer. The siren switched on again, only this time it was even louder.

"But there aren't even any fish in the tank!" yelled Teggs.

"Oh yes, there are," said Gipsy. A few deep-blue fish swam inside through the big hole. They came up to the front of the tank, as if to see what was happening. A few others came to join them. Then more. And more. Soon there were hundreds of fish staring at Gipsy through the glass.

They didn't seem very happy.

"Turn that siren off!" yelled Teggs. He
tried to bang his tail against the speaker, but
it was just out of reach.

"No way!" snapped the computer. "I'm
going to turn it *up*!" Sure enough, the siren
grew louder still.

"My ears are going to burst!" groaned Teggs.
He bashed the steel bars with his tail. They
sparked, but held firm. "We can't get out!"

"Never mind *us* getting *out*," said Gipsy fear-
fully. "Let's just hope those fish can't get *in*!"

"Fish? Why are you bothered by a few fish . . . ?"

But Teggs trailed off when he looked at the aquarium.

There were thousands of the tiny creatures now. They had banded together into one enormous group—a huge huddle of angry blue fish, moving and acting as one.

Floating all together, they made Mira seem like a minnow.

"That's the same shape I saw back at the

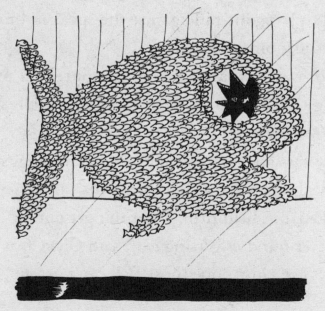

floating factory," cried Teggs over the earsplitting noise. "It wasn't a giant monster who sank the subs and chewed up the factories after all! It was these little fish—working together to *act* like a giant monster!"

Suddenly the dark, seething shape swept forward and smashed into the glass like a living battering ram.

"And now they want to get in here!" said Gipsy.

"But why?" Teggs asked. "What have we done?"

The thousands of fish opened their little mouths and gnashed at the glass. The crack in the side of the tank grew wider.

"Their teeth are as sharp as sharks'!" Gipsy gasped. "I think they're going to eat *us*!"

Chapter Nine

FIN-ISHED?

The great mass of little blue fish attacked the side of the tank again. The crack spread into a pattern of crazy zigzags, stretching from floor to ceiling.

"Look out, Gipsy!" shouted Teggs. "They're coming through!"

The fish hurled themselves at the glass, and the tank burst open. Teggs and Gipsy watched helplessly as the tiny creatures swarmed inside the larder . . .

. . . and ignored them completely.

Instead, the fish headed for the speaker in the ceiling, attacking it and tearing it open with their vicious teeth. The sound of the siren faded.

"Under attack!" gasped the computer voice. "The whisperfish have escaped the larder! Assistance needed—"

With a flash of sparks and an electronic

cough, the voice and the siren shut off altogether.

Teggs's and Gipsy's ears rang in the sudden silence.

The next second, the "monster" vanished as all the fish swam swiftly away in different directions. A few of them hung about in the larder, their little mouths opening and closing. But the others were already swimming back out to sea as if nothing had happened.

"Of course!" yelled Teggs at the top of his voice. But some of the fish gave him a nasty look, so he quickly shut up. "They weren't after us. They were after whatever was making the noise!"

"I don't get it," frowned Gipsy.

"You were right," he went on. "The cryptoclidus did disturb something when they built their factories here in the south—those whisperfish! Whisperfish must *hate* noise!"

Gipsy nodded slowly. "Well, the glass in that tank was very thick," she said. "I'll bet it made things very quiet in there."

"And once the ship crashed and they escaped, the ocean must have been quiet too," Teggs went on. "Until the cryptoclidus started building in whisperfish waters!"

"Of course!" cried Gipsy. "Ever since then,

these whisperfish have been joining together to chew up anything that makes a loud noise—floating factories, submarines, that silly siren. And once they've stopped the racket, they split up again."

"And so the 'monster' seems to vanish!" Teggs nodded. "That's why the whisperfish left us alone in our nice quiet shuttle and the silent diving bell. *We* weren't disturbing them!"

"Well, now we know what's been going on," said Gipsy. "But what good does it do us? We're almost out of air."

Teggs nodded. He felt a bit dizzy. "If we're not rescued soon . . ."

As he spoke, a massive, dark

shape swam up to them through the shattered tank.

"Oh no," groaned Teggs.

It was Mira!

"Coo-eee!" he said, waving a flipper. "I've been looking everywhere for you two! Now, it's my turn to hide . . ." He trailed off. "Wait a moment. This is my spaceship! What are you doing inside my spaceship?"

"Trying to get out," cried Gipsy.

But then a bright yellow light shone in at them through the glass.

"Don't tell me it's *another* monster!" Teggs groaned.

"It's . . . it's some kind of supersubmarine!" gasped Gipsy in surprise.

A gleaming sub was gliding through the water toward them.

Mira spun around to see. Then he scowled. "It's those flippery things!" he shouted. "They want to catch us! Well, I'll show them a thing or two!"

With that, he streaked out of the tank and over to the sub. His jaws were wide open.

Teggs stared in horror. "No, Mira, don't!"

But as Mira bit down on the nose of the sub—*Zzzzap!*

His eyes bulged. Then he stuck out his tongue, closed his eyes, and fell quietly to the seabed.

A hatch opened on top of the sub and Cripes swam out. Gipsy hugged Teggs with relief.

"So you did hear our SOS signal," said Teggs weakly.

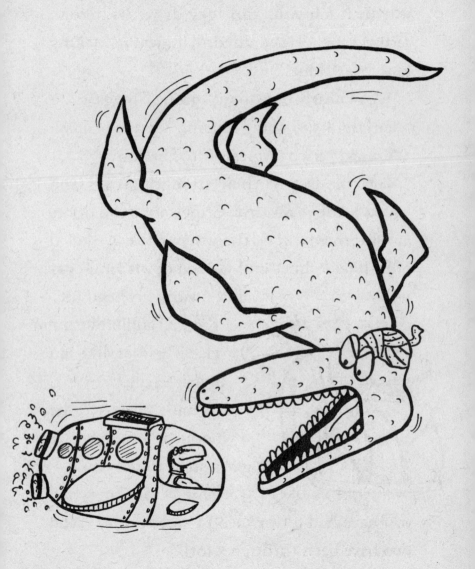

Cripes nodded. "Arx worked out the best way to reach you, and Iggy drove us here in record time!" He nodded. "Uh, you're looking kind of . . . blue!"

"We're nearly out of air," gasped Teggs.

"I'm think I'm going to faint," croaked Gipsy.

"Quick!" cried Cripes. "Into the sub!"

With the last of their strength, Teggs and Gipsy made it aboard. Cripes shut the doors and led them out of the water. Gipsy wriggled out of her helmet and gulped down air. Teggs just swung his head into the wall and broke the glass helmet like an oversized egg.

"That's better," he whooped. "And have we got a story to tell you!"

"Tell me about it when you have had a rest," said Cripes gently. "You two have been through a lot!"

"What happened to Mira?" asked Gipsy.

"He'll be all right," said Cripes. "He's just sleeping. When Iggy fixed the sub, he also gave it a special force field."

"Of course." Teggs beamed. "A force field's like a wall of solid energy. When Mira tried to bite it, he got a big shock!"

"Poor Mira," sighed Gipsy. "He's not really bad."

"We'll tow him back to Sea Station One," Teggs declared. "Then we can work out how to get him back home."

The sub's inner door opened and Iggy ran in. "Captain! Gipsy!" he beamed with delight. "You're all right!

"Just about," replied Gipsy. She gave Iggy a hug. "Though it's going to take *weeks* to get all the wrinkles out of my skin!"

A few hours later, the astrosaurs were safely back aboard Sea Station One. Teggs and Gipsy were both chilled to the bone from being in the freezing sea for so long. But after a lovely hot bath and a bucket of warm sea grass, they started to feel a bit better.

The sleeping Mira had been towed to a special undersea pen. The pen was locked up, and Cripes had placed guards there. A few hours later, the astrosaurs met Cripes on a balcony above the pen.

"No one is very happy about having a lio-pleurodon here at Sea Station One," grumbled Cripes.

"If he meant you any harm, don't you think he'd have attacked you already?" said Gipsy.

"I guess so," said Cripes. "Speaking of attacks, thanks for finding the truth behind our mysterious monster! Now all we have to do is catch all the whisperfish and they'll never bother us again."

Teggs gave Cripes a hard stare. "That doesn't seem fair."

"What do you mean?" asked Cripes.

"It can't be much fun being a whisperfish on the liopleurodon world," said Teggs. "Locked

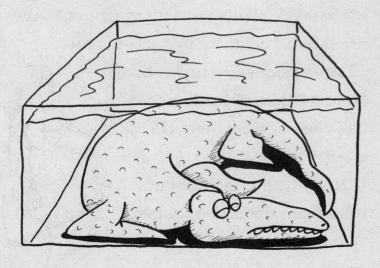

up in a tank and eaten for lunch—not much of a life, is it? But here on Aqua Minor, things are different. The whisperfish have enjoyed a peaceful life swimming freely in the sea for years." Teggs marched angrily up to Cripes. "And what do you want to do now? You want to catch them all and send them back home for supper!"

"But they're dangerous!" Cripes complained.

"All they want is some peace and quiet," said Arx. "They've never bothered you in the north. They probably won't bother you in the east and the west, either."

"Share the planet with them, Cripes," Teggs urged him. "Let them live here in peace."

Cripes nodded, a little shamefaced. "You're right. I'm sorry. Of course we'll let them stay!"

"*Hey!*" came a booming voice from the undersea pen. "What's going on here?"

"It's Mira," said Teggs. "He's woken up."

"But he sounds different," said Gipsy. "He sounds really scary!"

Suddenly Mira crashed through the surface of the water and glared up at them. "Who are you?" he bawled. "Who dares to lock *me* up?"

"Don't you recognize us?" asked Gipsy.

"Never seen you before!" he shouted. "I'm hungry! What have you done with my whisperfish?"

"They're off the menu," Teggs told him. "Sorry!"

"Sorry? You will be!" snarled the liopleurodon. "I'm Admiral Don Leo of the Liopleurodon Space Fleet! The last thing I remember is crash-landing on this crummy planet during a test flight," His eyes narrowed. "And I'm very, very *angry*!"

Chapter Ten

ALL WRAPPED UP!

Arx cleared his throat. "It would seem that the liopleurodon's memory has returned," he said. "It must be the shock he got from the force field."

"No one keeps me locked up!" roared Don Leo. "Forget the whisperfish—I'll eat every one of *you* when I get out of here!"

"Oh, dear," sighed Teggs. "We've dealt with one monster. Now here's another one to take its place!"

"There's not a prison built that can hold me!" growled Don Leo. "And I'll prove it!" He swam at top speed toward the side of the pen and bashed it over and over. The wall was thick, but soon cracks were starting to show.

Cripes was trembling. "He's going to get out into the open sea! Think of the damage he could cause!"

"We'll just have to stop him," said Teggs simply. "Cripes, Iggy, let's head for the super-sub—fast!"

With a final roar of rage, Don Leo smashed a huge hole in the side of the pen.

"Now I'm going to eat everyone on this planet!" he yelled.

"Not so fast!" shouted Teggs from the supersub. "First you'll have to deal with a couple of astrosaurs!"

With that, Iggy turned the supersub around and revved the dung-powered engines right in Don Leo's furious face.

"That tastes revolting!" Don Leo spluttered. "I'll get you for that!"

The supersub sped away with the liopleurodon hot on its heels.

"All right, Cripes," said Teggs. "Where's the nearest floating factory?"

"About three miles north," said Cripes. "But it's a brand-new building. We've only just put all the machines in."

"Perfect!" cried Teggs. "Well away from the whisperfish. Iggy, get us there at top speed!"

"Aye, aye, Captain." Iggy grinned.

But though the supersub roared through the saltwater at a blistering speed, Don Leo was gaining on them.

"We must keep ahead of him, Iggy!" urged Teggs.

Cripes pointed to a big block of metal ahead of them. "There's the floating factory!"

"Does it have a packing room?" asked Teggs. "You know, like the one I got trapped in on the wreck?"

"Sure it does," said Cripes. "Iggy, head for the intake pipe around the side. It'll take you straight there. But I still don't see—"

"No time for explanations now," said Teggs as they shot into the pipe and into the loading area. "I'm getting off! Park the sub and wait for me."

"But Don Leo's right behind us!" protested Iggy. "If he sees you, he'll eat you!"

"I hope he *tries*." Teggs smiled. "My plan depends on it!"

Iggy parked the supersub in the water just outside the packing room. As it bobbed on the surface of the water, Teggs jumped out and quickly waded over to another large pipe half-filled with water. Designed to let through tons of shelled ammonites for packing, it was easily big enough to fit a stegosaurus.

And with a bit of a squeeze, a livid liopleurodon.

Don Leo suddenly burst out of the water, ready to bite. His terrifying teeth missed Teggs's neck by millimeters.

"Phew!" Teggs whistled. "You know, I think

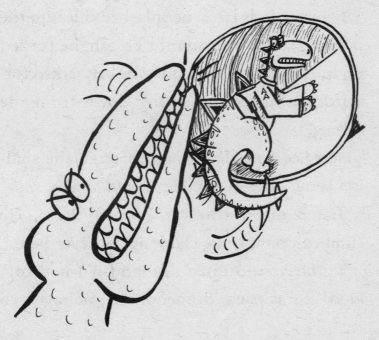

I liked Mira a whole lot better than Don Leo!"

"I'll like you a whole lot better when you're lining my stomach!" growled Don Leo.

"Don't hold your breath," said Teggs. He bashed Don Leo on the nose with his tail.

"Come here!" Don Leo roared in anger.

Teggs waded off down the pipe, with the liopleurodon slithering right behind him, trying to squeeze through.

A few seconds later, he splashed out into the packing room. Panting for breath, he turned on the machines. The conveyor belt jerked forward. Metal scoops swung down from the ceiling.

Don Leo wriggled along through the shallow water after Teggs. He looked *furious*.

"Catch me if you can!" cried Teggs. He climbed up onto the clanking conveyor belt.

"I'd chase you onto dry land if I had to!" Don Leo snarled. Somehow he managed to

flip himself out of the water and onto the
conveyor belt behind Teggs.

Now they were both heading straight for the
wrapping machine.

Don Leo laughed nastily. "I've got you now,
you stupid stegosaur!"

Teggs just smiled. "Actually, I think you'll
find *I've got you*!"

Just before he could fall into the wrapping
machine, Teggs jumped off the conveyor belt.
He hit the water safely with an enormous
splash. But it was too late for Don Leo. He

couldn't flip himself out of the way in time.

"No!" yelled the liopleurodon as he tumbled into the wrapping machine.

Teggs held his breath as the machine rattled and shook. Then it bulged like a balloon. Steam started to spurt from its insides.

But finally, out popped Don Leo, all wrapped up on a long plastic tray. Only his head, tail, and flippers were left sticking out.

"Get me out of here!" yelled the liopleurodon, struggling furiously.

But the conveyor belt moved him quickly on. He was tipped into a large wooden crate. Robot arms placed the lid on top and nailed it in place. Finally the crate was shoved off into the water with a big splash.

"There," said Teggs, "that should hold you till you've calmed down a bit!"

"What about my ship?" came Don Leo's muffled voice.

"I think your test flight is over," said Teggs. "That ship will never fly again. But your crew are still safely sleeping. If you promise to be good, I'm sure the crypto- clidus will help you all get back home to your own planet."

"And what if we're *not* good?" said Don Leo.

"I was sent here by the Dinosaur Space Service. They'll be watching you very closely," Teggs said sternly. "If you know what's good for you . . . behave!"

Just then Iggy and Cripes splashed into the packing room.

"You did it!" Iggy beamed.

"At last we can get on with our fishing in peace," said Cripes.

"As soon as you've helped Don Leo and his friends get back home," said Teggs. "But don't worry. I think he'll be better behaved from now on!"

"Suppose so," grumbled Don Leo from his crate.

"Well, I think that about *wraps things up* here." Teggs chuckled. He spoke into his communicator. "Arx? Gipsy? It's Teggs. Mission accomplished!"

Gipsy's voice crackled out: "Well done, Captain!"

"Admiral Rosso will be delighted!" added Arx.

"Get the shuttle ready," Teggs ordered. "Then let's all grab dinner somewhere *dry*." He grinned at Iggy. "I'm ready for a ten-course banquet—with a big, new adventure for dessert!"

The Mind-Swap Menace

GET A SNEAK PEAK HERE!

It took less than a minute for the shuttle to reach the space station. Teggs and Iggy put on their space suits and climbed in through the big hole in the side. They found themselves in a gloomy corridor.

"Let's have a quick look around," said Teggs. "Just in case anyone's been hurt."

"If there are any meat-eaters still on this station, *we* could get hurt!" said Iggy. Even so, he followed his captain along the dark passage without hesitation.

The station was a grim, forbidding place. It was made of metal and was thick with shadows. To their right, stars shone a ghostly light through small, barred windows set high in the outer wall. To their left was a line of huge, heavy doors, covered in bolts and locks.

Teggs tried one of them. The door creaked open into a cramped room with just a bed and bucket inside. It looked like some kind of jail cell.

"Iggy? I think this place was a prison," said

Teggs. "A lockup for carnivore criminals."

Iggy agreed. "Pretty *dangerous* criminals too, from the size of those locks!"

"We won't hang about," said Teggs. "Let's get the beacon working and go back to the *Sauropod*."

Iggy took the bulky beacon from his captain's back. It looked like a large red triangle with a flashing blue light on the top and didn't take long to set up.

"There," said Iggy. "That will send out warning signals to any passing ships, telling them to keep out of the way."

Teggs grinned at him. "Next stop, Diplos! Come on."

But the cell door wouldn't open.

"Funny," said Teggs. "Must be stuck."

"But we left it open so we could move about!" Iggy remembered. "There's hardly room in here to swing a compsognathus!"

Teggs nodded grimly. "So either it swung

shut behind us and jammed—or someone has locked us in!"

A nasty snigger came from the other side of the door. Then a white, wispy gas started pumping through the keyhole.

"Hold your breath, Iggy!" Teggs gasped. "We've walked into a trap!"